Sleeping Beauty

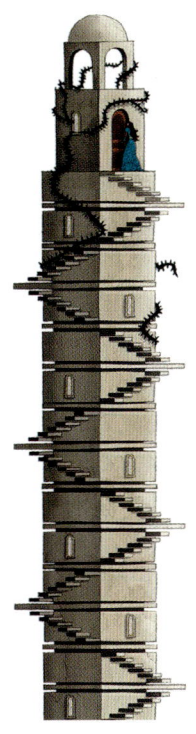

Written by
Rachel Rooney

Illustrated by
Dani Padron

Collins

Once upon a time and far away
in a castle, lived a king and queen.
They feasted on the finest food and drink
and wore the finest clothes you've ever seen.

They had all the riches in the kingdom.
Diamonds, sapphires, rubies by the tonne.
But what they really wanted most of all
was a baby daughter, or a son.

The queen fell ill, so the doctor came.
She was lying sick and tired in bed.
He smiled at her, "I'm very pleased to say
that you'll be a mother soon," he said.

"I am so excited!" cried the queen.
The king said, "I'm the happiest man on Earth!"
The servants rushed around like little mice
to get the castle ready for the birth.

The royal wish came true a few months later
just as the sun rose up to end the night.
A healthy baby girl was born that morning –
she came with the dawning of the light.

"She is called Aurora," said the queen.
"A perfect name for our new princess."
"We must have a party," said the king.
"It will be the biggest and the best."

The queen agreed. She hugged Aurora close
and sang a sleepy song into her ear.
The king went off to make a party list
of every friend they knew from far and near.

The most important of the party guests
were seven fairies with their magic powers.
The king had lots of other friends to ask.
The list grew long. It took him many hours.

He invited hundreds to the party,
in letters written carefully by hand.
He put them in a sack and sent them off
to all the lucky houses in the land.

When they read the letters the next morning the people shouted out, "Hip hip hooray! We'll meet the princess at the castle." They started to get ready straight away.

The royal cook prepared a massive feast. He served it up on polished golden plates. A band began to play some jolly tunes. The footmen opened up the castle gates.

Outside, there was a noisy crowd of people
each waiting with a present for the child.
One by one they went into the castle.
The happy queen shook every hand and smiled.

There were fresh, red roses on the tables.
Music floated gently round the hall.
Everybody ate and laughed and chatted.
It was the finest party of them all.

The seven magic fairies sat together
around a table with the queen and king.
When the feast had ended, one stood up,
"It's time to tell you of the gift I bring ...

I give the gift of beauty to this girl.
More beautiful than any shining pearl."

The second said, "Then I will add to it
a brain that's full of cleverness and wit."

"I will give her music," said the third,
"to play the flute as sweetly as a bird."

Fairy number four said, "I have brought
a gift to make her shine at dance and sport."

"I give," said the fifth, "a heart so pure that she will love and laugh for evermore."

The sixth one said, "And I have brought along the gift of words – for poetry and song."

But as the seventh fairy stood to speak,
Another fairy burst into the room.
She hadn't been invited to the party
and in her anger, cast a spell of doom.

She gave a wicked laugh and waved her wand.
"Your daughter will not reach sixteen," she said.
"Beware! A spinning wheel will end her life.
One little needle prick, and she'll be dead."

The angry fairy turned and walked away.
The queen went pale and she began to cry.
So fairy number seven used her powers
to make quite sure Aurora wouldn't die.

"It will not be her death. Please do not weep.
Instead, she'll spend a hundred years asleep."

The king looked high and low for spinning wheels.
He chopped them up and set them all ablaze.
When the fire died down, they all forgot
the angry fairy and her wicked ways.

As time went by, Princess Aurora grew into the girl the fairies said she'd be. Everybody loved the young princess. Life was good, and they lived happily.

One day, aged fifteen, she was left alone,
and so decided that she would explore.
She climbed the winding staircase of the tower
and opened up a little wooden door.

Inside, she saw an old maid spinning wool
and asked her, "May I have a quick turn, too?"
Reaching out, the needle pricked her hand.
As it did, the fairy's spell came true.

Aurora yawned and rubbed her tired eyes.
She sank into a deep sleep on the ground.
Soon the sleepy spell began to spread
till nothing in the castle made a sound.

The king and queen sat dozing on their thrones.
The royal cook sat dreaming in his chair.
Dogs and cats were snoozing side by side.
The cuckoo in the clock stopped in mid-air.

While they slept, a wood of prickly thorns grew up around the castle, tall and wide. They grew and grew until they reached the top, hiding it, and all who lived inside.

Stories of the beautiful princess
were told across the land, by candlelight.
People tried to reach her, one by one.
They battled in the thorns but lost the fight.

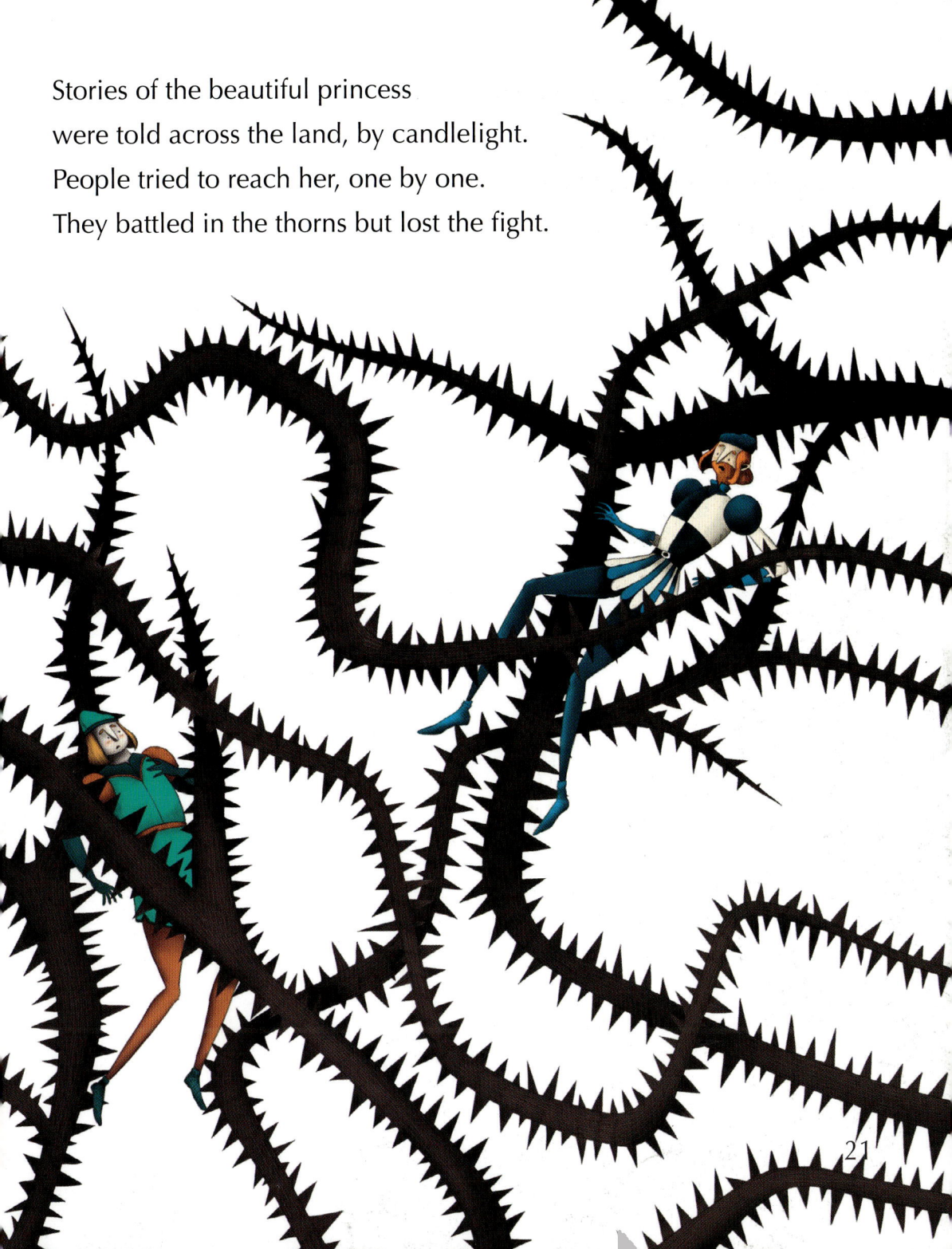

A hundred years passed by and then a prince
set off upon his journey to the wood.
Like the princess, he was handsome, strong
bright, poetic, musical and good.

A thousand prickly thorns tore at his clothes.
A thousand thorns and more dug into his skin.
But still, he carried onwards through the dark
to find the sweet princess who slept within.

Finally, he reached the castle gates.
He pushed them open, had a look around.
The footmen in the hall were quietly snoring.
A butler was asleep upon the ground.

He searched inside the dining room, the kitchen
and all the royal bedrooms he could find.
He spied a wooden door up in the tower
and opened it to see what lay behind.

On the floor, he saw Princess Aurora,
more beautiful than all the stories said.
His heart began to thump inside his chest,
and thoughts began to race around his head.

At last, the fairy's spell began to break.
Aurora yawned and opened up her eyes.
Above, she saw a handsome, scruffy boy.
A dreamy prince dressed in a torn disguise.

Princess Aurora stretched her sleepy arms.
A hundred years of rest had made her weak.
The prince held out his hand and helped her up.
Aurora smiled and kissed him on the cheek.

"I'm so pleased to meet you," said the prince.
"I'm pleased to meet you, too," said the princess.
In that moment, they both fell in love.
They had never felt such happiness.

Below, the king and queen were waking up.
And the footmen, cook and butler too.
Dogs and cats began to bark and hiss.
The cuckoo in the clock called out, "Cuckoo!"

Aurora took the prince to meet her parents.
He told them all about the fairy's spell.
They listened to his tale and rubbed their eyes.
The queen said, "Gosh!" The king said, "Well, well, well!"

Life went back the way it was before.
The castle filled again with love and laughter.
Princess Aurora and her prince were wed.
And everyone was happy, ever after.

Once upon a time and far away
in a castle, lived a king and queen.
They feasted on the finest food and drink
and wore the finest clothes you've ever seen ...

Making a spell

"I give the gift of beauty to this girl."

"I will add to it a brain that's full of cleverness and wit."

"I will give her music, to play the flute as sweetly as a bird."

"I have brought a gift to make her shine at dance and sport."

"I give a heart so pure that she will love and laugh for evermore."

"I have brought along the gift of words – for poetry and song."

"Beware! A spinning wheel will end her life. One little needle prick, and she'll be dead."

Breaking a spell

She sank into a deep sleep
on the ground.

They battled in the thorns but lost the fight.

He spied a wooden door
up in the tower.

The prince held out his
hand and helped her up.

Ideas for reading

Written by Clare Dowdall, PhD
Lecturer and Primary Literacy Consultant

Reading objectives:
- read books that are structured in different ways
- increase familiarity with a wide range of books including fairy stories and retell orally
- make predictions from details stated and applied

Spoken language objectives:
- ask relevant questions to extend their understanding and knowledge
- participate in discussions, presentations, performances, role play, improvisations and debates

Curriculum links:
PSHE – feeling excluded

Resources:
art materials for invitations, ICT for recording a performance.

Build a context for reading

- Ask children to recall what they know about the story *Sleeping Beauty*. Who are the main characters? What kind of story is it?
- Look at the front cover and read the blurb aloud. Discuss the fairytale features (narrator's voice, rhyme, fairy story language), and the features that might appear in this story (characters, events, settings etc.)
- Ask children to suggest what will happen to the king and queen who enjoy such a fine life, based on the information in the blurb.

Understand and apply reading strategies

- Turn to pp2-5. Invite the children to join in as you read the verses aloud, emphasising using expression rhythm and rhyme to perform the reading.
- Discuss how this story is structured, using verses and rhyme.
- Ask children to continue reading, taking a verse each. Support them to read with expression rhythm and rhyme.